Mac is a happy puppy dog.
He always has fun!

One day he wanted more adventure so he decided to go for a hike.

He followed a path that was marked with a New York State hiking trail sign.

It went into the woods

and over a stream.

The trail went up a hill.
The trail became very steep
and there were lots of rocks.
He walked all morning.

He saw interesting moss, mushrooms and bugs.

He stopped to rest on a big rock
at the end of the trail.

He looked and saw that he was on top of an Adirondack mountain. Everything below looked so small.

He liked it so much
he decided to camp overnight.

He collected sticks to make
a shelter and a campfire.

He ate blueberries and nuts, but
Mac wished he had marshmallows too.

When nighttime came, the sky was filled with stars. There were more than Mac could count.

In the morning he saw the sun rise.
That was cool.

Then he hiked home.
There's nothing quite like the fresh outdoors.
It makes Mac a very happy dog.

But there's always the comfort of home to enjoy when you get back.